Tale Twisters

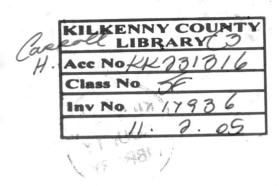

Rigby, Halley Court, Jordan Hill, Oxford, OX2 8EJ
a division of Reed Educational and Professional Publishing Ltd
www.rigbyed.co.uk

Rigby is a registered trademark of Reed Educational and Professional
Publishing Ltd

Tale Twisters first published 2002

Series editor: Wendy Wren

06 05 04
10 9 8 7 6 5 4

Tale Twisters	ISBN 0433 07695 X
Group Reading Pack with Teaching Notes	ISBN 0433 07701 8

Illustrated by Nick Schon, Jonathan Allen, Delphine Thomas
Cover illustration © Max Ellis 2002
Repro by Digital Imaging, Glasgow
Printed in Great Britain by Ashford Colour Press, Gosport, Hants.

WHO DID THAT?

by Leon Rosselson

One Monday morning, we were all
in the classroom ready to do some
painting. Mrs Morgan always put
some of our paintings on the walls to
brighten up the room. Our school
was quite old and Mrs Morgan said it
was about time our classroom had a
new lick of paint. The walls were a
dirty cream colour and the paint on
the ceiling was starting to flake.

3

While I was waiting, I looked around the room. I could smell the purple and white flowers on Mrs Morgan's desk. I could see the hamster running on his wheel and next to him was a globe of the world. On the table where we put interesting things, I could see shells, pretty stones and some old coins. Last week, Barney brought in a dead pigeon and put it on the table. Mrs Morgan told him to take it out and throw it in the dustbin. Barney was always doing things like that.

Mrs Morgan was small and thin and wore glasses. She put a big rosy apple on her desk.

"Now you can all see what this is," she said, cutting the apple in half.

"An elephant," called out Barney. We all giggled.

"Don't be silly, Barney," sighed Mrs Morgan. She explained that we had to paint the apple. "Red for the skin. White for the flesh. Black for the stalk. Brown for the pips. Paint it carefully. I've got to go out for a moment but I'll hear if you make a noise."

After a little while, Mrs Morgan came
back into the classroom. She stared at
the two halves of the apple on the
table. They had turned black with
yellow spots, as if they had caught a
terrible disease. Mrs Morgan's face went
as red as a beetroot.

"Who did that?" she shouted.

"Not me, Miss," I said.

"Not me, Miss," said Gary.

"Not me, Miss," said Rifat.

"Not me, Miss," said Lily.

"Not me, Miss," said everyone,
except Barney.

The whole class turned to look at Barney, who was staring into space.

"Come here, Barney," ordered Mrs Morgan.

"I was only painting the apple like you said, Miss," mumbled Barney.

Mrs Morgan made him sit by himself in the corner for the rest of the lesson. He had to sit with half a black and spotty apple on his head. He did look silly.

On Tuesday, we had maths. Mrs Morgan told us we were going to learn about taking away.

"I'll have a burger and chips," shouted Barney.

"Do be quiet, Barney," scolded Mrs Morgan. "Now I'll give each table ten cubes. I want you to work in pairs. One of you can take a certain number of cubes away and the other one can say how many cubes are left."

Mrs Morgan went round the tables to make sure we knew what we were doing. When she got back to her desk, she saw that the door of the hamster's cage was open. The hamster was gone. Mrs Morgan's face went as white as mashed potato.

"Who did that?" she shouted, pointing at the hamster's cage.

"Not me, Miss," I said.

"Not me, Miss," said Gary.

"Not me, Miss," said Rifat.

"Not me, Miss," said Lily.

"Not me, Miss," said everyone, except Barney.

The whole class turned to look at Barney, who was hiding behind a comic.

"Stand up, Barney," ordered Mrs Morgan.

When Barney stood up, we could see the hamster's head poking out from his pocket.

"I was only practising taking away like you said, Miss," mumbled Barney.

Mrs Morgan took away his comic and made him sit by himself for the rest of the morning. He did look lonely.

On Wednesday, our teacher put a bowl of water on every table.

"Today," she explained, "we're going to learn about water."

"It's wet," piped up Barney. We all giggled.

"Be careful, Barney," warned Mrs Morgan. "Now I want you to see which things float and which things sink. I'm sure you all know that a boat will float, but what about a brick?"

We were all busy when, suddenly, there was an enormous splash. Water whooshed up everywhere. Mrs Morgan's face went as purple as an aubergine.

"Who did that?" she shouted.

"Not me, Miss," I said.

"Not me, Miss," said Gary.

"Not me, Miss," said Rifat.

"Not me, Miss," said Lily.

"Not me, Miss," said everyone, except Barney.

We all turned to look at Barney. He was standing on his chair waving one foot in the air.

"I was only trying to float my boot like you said, Miss," mumbled Barney.

Mrs Morgan made him wipe up the water. He had to stay in all day with one boot on and one boot off. He did look sorry for himself.

On Thursday, Barney didn't do anything naughty or silly for the whole day.

"I'll give you five minutes to make everything neat and tidy," said Mrs Morgan, at five to three. "Otherwise, there'll be no story."

Everyone rushed around collecting rubbers, scissors and paper. We threw rubbish into the waste-paper bin, sharpened pencils, wiped tables and put everything back in its box. When the boxes were on Mrs Morgan's table, we waited for her to tell us a story.

Mrs Morgan looked at one of the boxes and her face went as green as a cabbage. She picked up a pencil, then another one and another one. She held them up, glaring at the class. They were so small you could hardly see them.

"Who did that?" she demanded.
"Not me, Miss," I said.
"Not me, Miss," said Gary.
"Not me, Miss," said Rifat.
"Not me, Miss," said Lily.
"Not me, Miss," said everyone, except Barney.

The whole class turned to look at Barney, who was sitting staring into the distance.

"Barney! Come here!" rapped out Mrs Morgan.

"I only sharpened the pencils to make them neat and tiny, Miss," mumbled Barney. "Like you said."

Mrs Morgan sent him out of the room so he couldn't hear the story. He did look sad.

On Friday, Mrs Morgan told us we were going to have a special music lesson.

"Mr Hunter is coming," Mrs Morgan went on, "and he's bringing a trumpet with him. Now, who wants to learn the trumpet?"

"Me, Miss," I said.

"Me, Miss," said Gary.

"Me, Miss," said Rifat.

"Me, Miss," said Lily.

"Me, Miss," said everyone, except Barney.

"Well, you can't all learn," Mrs Morgan said. "Mr Hunter will see which of you can play a note on the trumpet."

There was a murmur of excitement when Mr Hunter came in for the music lesson. He showed us how to blow a note on the trumpet. We all tried puffing and blowing as hard as we could but the only sound we made was like the wind blowing through a tunnel.

When it was Barney's turn, out came the loudest, rudest, funniest raspberry noise you ever heard. Mrs Morgan looked up from her work.

"Who did that?" she asked.

"Not me, Miss," I said.

"Not me, Miss," said Gary.

"Not me, Miss," said Lily.

"Not me, Miss," said everyone, except Barney.

The whole class turned to look at Barney. He was staring at the trumpet, with his mouth wide open.

"Well done, Barney!" exclaimed Mrs Morgan. "You can be the first one in the school to learn the trumpet."

A big grin lit up Barney's face. He did look pleased.

What's That Smell?

by Jonathan Allen

The sun was shining brightly. The sky was blue. The birds were singing. It was a beautiful spring day. Mr Matthews smiled as he flung open the window. Just as he took a deep breath of air, a heavy lorry thundered past the house.

"Urgh!" He pulled a face and gasped as a cloud of diesel fumes blew up towards him. He quickly shut the window again.

From inside the house Mr Matthews gazed out at the spring sunshine bathing the street outside. He smiled again but then he noticed three large bin bags by the corner shop. They had burst open and a scruffy dog was nosing through and eating all the scraps it could find. Next to the bin bags was a heap of broken glass and an old window frame. A van had parked outside the shop and was blocking the road. The people in cars stuck behind the van were tooting their horns loudly.

Mr Matthews pulled another face. "Right!" he said. "Time we all went for a nice drive in the country!"

"Uh?" said Sarah, looking up from her computer.

"Aw!" said Callum, "there's snooker on the telly."

"Well, that's probably the best reason I can think of to go out," said Mr Matthews as he turned off the television. "You can watch snooker anytime! Look! It's a beautiful spring day. Beautiful spring days don't come around that often. The place to be on a beautiful spring day is out in the country! Away from all the fumes and the noise of the town."

Sarah and Callum groaned but they didn't really mind all that much. They were a bit bored with sitting at home and quite liked going on trips to the countryside. Not that they would ever tell their dad that!

"We should have made a picnic," said Sarah as they got into the car.

"No need," said Mr Matthews. "There will be lots of places to eat. It will only take us about forty minutes to get into some lovely countryside. Just in time for lunch."

There was quite a lot of traffic but it did not take them long to reach the edge of town. The traffic lights all seemed to be on green and there were no road-works to hold them up. The spring sunshine was beaming down on everyone and everything.

Children were playing in the park. Some people were walking dogs and others were sitting on the grass chatting to each other.

The High Street was full of bright colours gleaming in the spring light – fruit and vegetables, cans and boxes, posters and billboards gleamed in the sunshine. Mr Matthews hummed happily as he drove along.

"Dad, are we nearly there yet?" asked Sarah.

"Not long now!" replied Mr Matthews, as they left the town behind them. Callum and Sarah grunted, not really listening. Callum was reading a comic. Sarah was trying to make her front tooth wobble with her tongue. It was definitely a bit loose.

"Hooray! Here we are in the countryside!" cried Mr Matthews as they swept over the top of a hill. "Look at that view!"

The children looked. They had to admit it was very pretty. Green and brown and white with woods and a river and farms.

"Cool!" said Callum.

"Neat!" agreed Sarah.

"I'm hungry," said Callum. "When can we eat?"

"Soon," said Mr Matthews. "Just smell that clean air!" he said, winding down his window as he turned off into a side road. "This is a lovely little road. Hardly anyone knows about it. I used to come out here with your mother. In fact, just round this corner you'll see a . . . arghh!" He braked sharply. A farmer with a stick was standing in the road holding up the traffic. Black and white cows were being herded out of a field by a man on a tractor. They crowded into the road ahead, mooing loudly.

There were now several other cars behind them and in front of them the old tractor was belting out clouds of evil-smelling diesel fumes.

"Urgh!" coughed Mr Matthews as he quickly rolled his window up. "Look at the lovely cows!" he said, trying to make the best of it. The children grunted. Callum went back to his comic and Sarah tried to make her tooth wobble again.

It was a big herd of cows, so it seemed ages before the road was clear. The smoky tractor turned off into the next field. With a sigh of relief Mr Matthews wound down his window again.

"Just down this road there is a lovely country pub where we can have lunch. We can sit outside and breathe the clean, country air," said Mr Matthews.

He drove around the next bend into another hold-up. There were road-works, there were cars and there were traffic lights. They were on red, of course.

"Dad?" cried Sarah suddenly. "What's that awful smell?"

"Pooh! Yeah!" said Callum. "What is it?"

"Just an everyday country smell!" said Mr Matthews brightly. He was trying to pretend he didn't mind it. "I expect it's that pig farm down there. I'll shut my window if you like. . ." He quickly rolled the window up.

"Dad?" said Callum, "we've been in the countryside for exactly one hour and twenty minutes. All we've done is sit in traffic and nearly choke to death twice. What happened to the clean air and empty roads?"

"Yeah, and we haven't had anything to eat," moaned Sarah.

"All right!" said Mr Matthews, "Look on the bright side. Enjoy the lovely sunshine. The lights will change in a minute and the pub is just down the road."

"Dad?"

"What is it, Sarah?"

"The sun's just gone in!"

Mr Matthews groaned once more.

"And it's raining!" put in Callum, just in case Mr Matthews hadn't seen the big drops that were starting to trickle down the windscreen.

"Are these traffic lights stuck on red or something?" Sarah wanted to know. "We've been here ages!"

Mr Matthews sighed deeply. "I'm sorry this hasn't worked out," he said at last.

"That's all right, Dad," said Sarah.

"It's not your fault," said Callum. "You couldn't help the hold-ups and the smells."

"Thanks, kids," said Mr Matthews. He was starting to feel a bit better. "Right," he said, "I'm going to turn round and head back home. Back to the bright, friendly streets and the only slightly smelly air!"

"All right!" cried Callum and Sarah.

"You know what?" said Mr Matthews as they drove along.

"What?"

"If we hurry, we might catch the end of the snooker!"

The Ghost Train

by David Webb

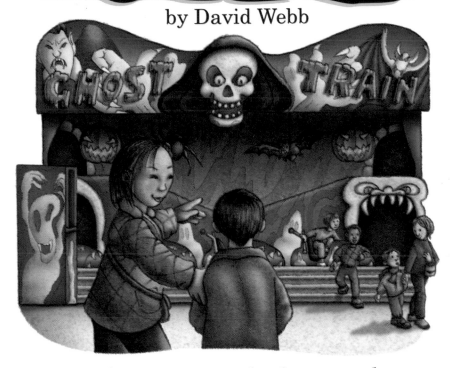

Lily and Tim were at the fairground, waiting to get on the Ghost Train. Suddenly, it rattled out of the dark tunnel and screeched to a halt right in front of them.

"I'm not sure," began Tim, as he stared at the ghosts painted on the side of the train. "I don't know if I'll like it."

"Don't be such a baby," said Lily. "There aren't real ghosts in there. There are only pretend ones."

"I know that but I'm not sure if I'll like it, Lily," said Tim.

"We're only allowed one more ride and I want to go on the Ghost Train. Are you coming, or not?" Lily asked.

"I suppose so," said Tim, slowly.

He looked back towards the plastic tables and chairs outside the tea van. He waved feebly at their mum. She was sipping a drink from a white plastic cup and waved back at him.

"Come on, then," said Lily. She shoved her brother towards the nearest carriage.

They climbed onto the train and the attendant pushed down the safety bar.

"That will be a pound each," he said, putting out his hand for the money. Tim thought he looked weird. Thin strands of limp, grey hair hung loosely over his pale face. His sunken eyes stared straight ahead. Lily put the money into his bony hand but he did not say "thank you".

"It's all the late nights," explained Lily. "He probably only gets to sleep during the day."

"So did Dracula," said Tim. He was still unhappy. He just wanted the ride to begin, so that it would soon be over.

Nothing happened for a few minutes. The attendant walked up and down. A few more people climbed onto the train and he took their money. Tim and Lily peered into the dark tunnel ahead of them. When they looked around again, the attendant had disappeared.

"Strange," muttered Tim. "He was there a few seconds ago."

Just then, the carriage jerked forwards, towards the black opening of the tunnel.

"Can't change your mind now, can you?" said Lily. She grinned at her young brother. Tim really wanted to get off the train, but it was too late.

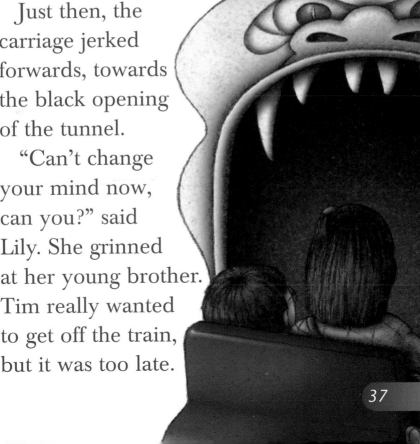

The carriage began to move quickly into the darkness. Tim took a deep breath and gripped the safety bar tightly. It was pitch black within seconds. At once there were squeals and screams from the carriages behind. Lily joined in with a screech of excitement that made Tim jump!

A sudden flash lit the darkness and Tim caught sight of a green, grinning skull. Something dropped from the tunnel roof and brushed against his face. It felt like a giant cobweb. The carriage slowed with a jerk. There was another lightning flash and a drumroll of thunder. A coffin sprang forward from the wall and Tim could see a mummy wrapped in white bandages.

Lily screamed and grabbed hold of her brother's arm.

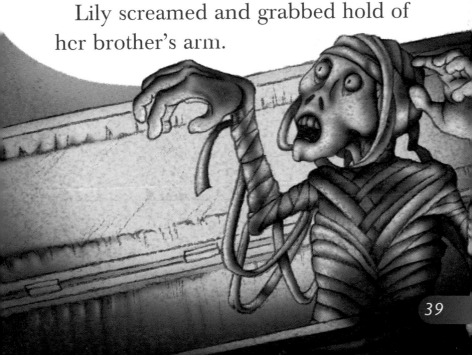

The Ghost Train began to move more quickly again. A cackle of witch-like laughter echoed in the tunnel.

"When will it stop? I want to get out!" yelled Lily, clinging onto her brother.

As soon as she said this, the train suddenly stuttered and then shuddered to a halt. There wasn't a sound. The squeals and the screams had stopped, and the silence was somehow more frightening.

"W–what's happening?" stammered Lily. "W–why have we stopped?"

"How should I know?" said Tim. "Maybe it's meant to happen. Maybe it's part of the ride."

"I don't think it's part of the ride, Tim. Something has gone wrong." Lily sounded frightened. "I don't like it, Tim."

They were in total darkness and there was a strange, eerie silence. It felt like the middle of the night. They sat very still in the dark silence and listened.

"Why is nothing happening?" whispered Lily. She didn't know why she was whispering. It just seemed the right thing to do. "I'm sure something has gone wrong."

A sudden shout from behind them made Lily jump and shudder with fear.

"Hel–lo–oh! Hello! Is anybody there?"

"It's all right," said Tim, patting his sister's arm. "It's only someone calling from one of the carriages behind us."

"Are you sure, Tim? Are you sure that's what it is?" whispered Lily.

"Well, I suppose it could be the mummy calling from its coffin," said Tim, slowly. He was beginning to enjoy himself.

"Shut up, Tim!" snapped Lily. "This is no time for jokes!"

There was another loud shout from behind them. Tim was just about to shout back when the strangest thing happened. They saw a small circle of light on the tunnel wall a few metres in front of them. It stayed quite still for a few moments. Then it started growing and then shrinking and then leaping forwards again.

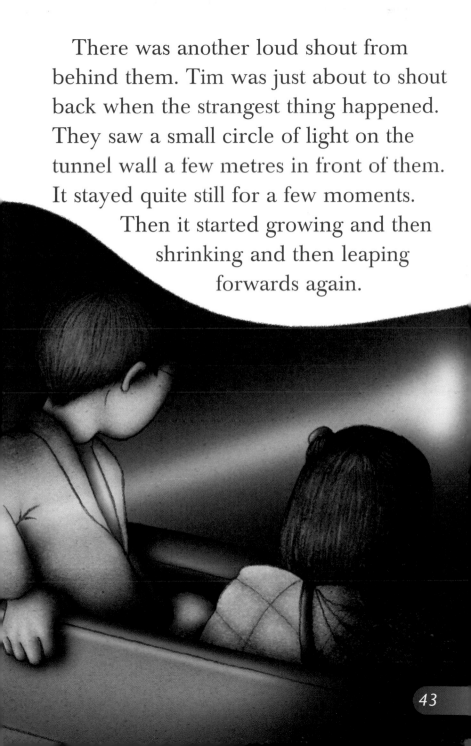

"Wh—what is it, Tim? Why is it leaping around the tunnel like that?" asked Lily, in a frightened voice.

"I'm not sure," said Tim. He wasn't frightened, but he was puzzled. "It looks like some kind of light."

"Well, I can see that!" snapped Lily. "I'm not stupid, you know. There's something in the tunnel, Tim. It's getting nearer."

The very next moment a face loomed out of the darkness. A deathly, pale face, with dark, sunken eyes that stared down at the two trapped children. Lily let out a scream which echoed through the tunnel over and over again. She clutched Tim more tightly than ever as the ghostly figure raised an arm.

"The train's stopped working," said the attendant, as he shone his torch towards the floor. "You'll have to follow me out of the tunnel."

Lily could not speak for a moment. She wiped the sweat from her face and then said, slowly, "The train has stopped working? We have to follow you out of the tunnel?"

"That's right," said the attendant. He lifted up the carriage safety bar. "Don't worry. You'll get your money back!"

"Come on, Tim," said Lily. She did not seem at all frightened now. "There's nothing to worry about."

A minute later, Tim and Lily walked out of the tunnel. It was very bright and noisy, after the darkness and silence inside. They rubbed their eyes and looked all around. Their mum was standing in the crowd by the exit. She was looking worried and she rushed across as soon as she saw them.

"Are you all right?" she asked. "Were you frightened, when the ride stopped?"

"Tim was very brave," said Lily, before her brother could speak. "I looked after him, of course."

The attendant handed the money back
to Lily. "If you come back tomorrow you
can have a free ride," he said, smiling.

"Great!" said Tim. "That was the best
ride I've ever been on!"

Lily took the money and stared at the
man. Were those fangs she had spotted
when his pale, deathly face had smiled?

"Thanks," said Lily, backing away.
"I'm not sure. We'll see. I quite fancy the
Big Wheel, actually."